Some of the nice things people have said about the first EMU Club adventure, *Alien Invasion in My Backyard*:

"The type of non-stop action and improbably hilarious fun that only a kid could dream up"
— GEEKDAD.COM

"Filled with wild twists and funny dialogue"
— PUBLISHERS WEEKLY

"The EMU Club inhabits exactly the world I always hoped to live in when I was 12, when the answer to questions like 'Where did I put my toy' led inevitably to alien conspiracies and secret underground tunnels. A book for the curious and adventurous!"
— CORY DOCTOROW, AUTHOR OF *LITTLE BROTHER*

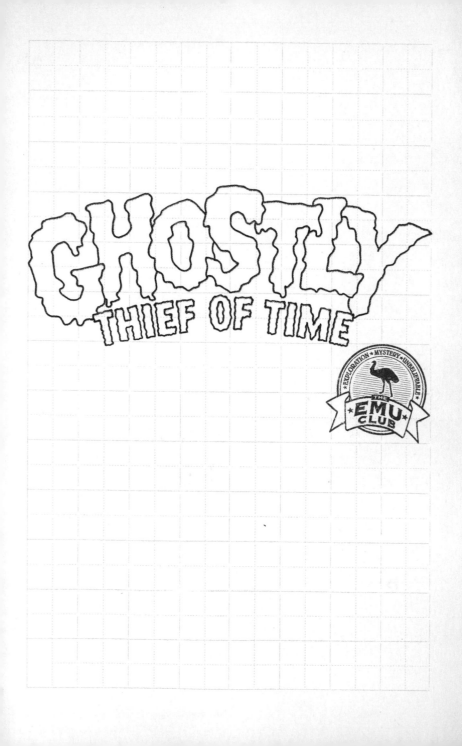

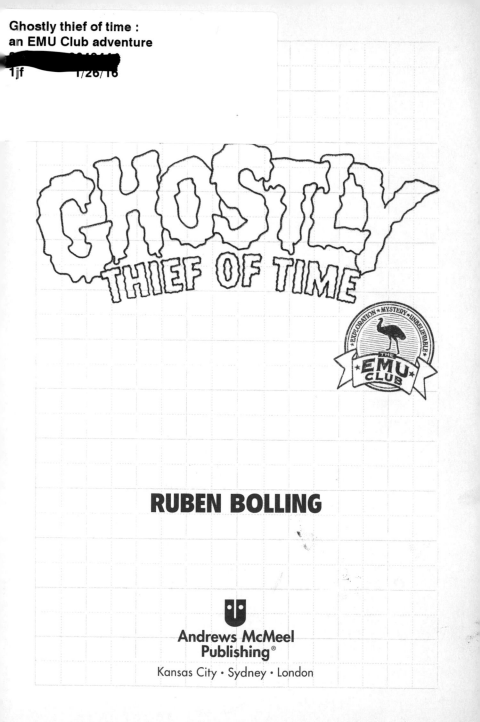

GHOSTLY THIEF OF TIME

EXPLORATION ★ MYSTERY ★ UNBELIEVABLE

THE EMU CLUB

RUBEN BOLLING

Andrews McMeel
Publishing®

Kansas City • Sydney • London

OFFICIAL EMU CLUB REPORT

PART ONE

THE PART AT THE BEGINNING OF EVERY EMU CLUB REPORT WHERE I MAKE SURE IT'S TOP SECRET

NOTICE:

TOP SECRET

FOR EMU CLUB EYES ONLY

DO NOT READ!

IF FOUND, RETURN TO STUART TENNEMEIER

CONFIDENTIAL

CLASSIFIED

PART TWO
THE PART WITH EMU CLUB BACKGROUND INFORMATION

Okay, this is the Official Report of the EMU Club's Second Adventure. For reference, the Official Report of the EMU Club's First Mystery has been filed in a shoe box in the back of my closet. Under a pile of old clothes that don't fit me anymore.

The Exploration-Mystery-Unbelievable Club (Code Name: EMU Club) was formed a couple of months ago by the following individuals:

$\longrightarrow$

Me. Stuart Tennemeier.

Age: 11

Code Name: WolfStalker

Rank: President

Skills: Improvisational martial arts (I can make up karate and kung fu moves very quickly). Leadership. "If you cross the line, he'll cross you out." (Which is a quote I made up for myself, like the ones you see on a movie poster for an action hero.)

Brian Hrznicz

Age: 11

Code Name: None

Rank: C.E.O. (second in command)

Skills: Loyally follows his leader. Follows orders. Hand washing. Superb organizational skills. Fast typist. Also, he's a pretty smart guy. Plays the didgeridoo. Also, thumb is double-jointed, which looks gross.

 Violet Tennemeier

Age: 8

Code Name: None

Rank: Photographer

Skills: None known. Sister of president (me). Arts and crafts. She wanted to put glitter on the cover page of this report. Yeah, right.

Ferdinand

Age: Unknown

Code Name: None

Rank: Sergeant at Arms

Skills: I may as well just come out and say this.
Ferdinand is my dog, and he's an alien robot.

So that's the team, and I don't like to brag,
but we pretty much saved the Earth from an alien
invasion over the summer. And after that
kind of adventure, we were looking for another
mystery to solve.

PART THREE
THE PART WHERE WE TRY TO THINK OF A NEW MYSTERY

It was the end of the summer, and Brian and I were sitting on the swings in my backyard. We don't actually swing on them anymore (we're not babies), but we often use them to sit and talk. And sometimes swing a little bit.

Brian said, "So what should our next mystery be, Stuart?"

I said, "You know, you could call me by my code name, 'WolfStalker.' You don't have to, but I think it might be a good idea in case anyone's listening."

"Look around," Brian said. "No one is listening. We are alone."

"You never know," I told him. Now that we were in the high-stakes world of intergalactic adventuring, you could never be too careful.

"All right, <u>WolfStalker</u>," Brian said, rolling his eyes. "What should our next case be?"

The eye roll definitely ruined the coolness of being called by my code name. "I don't know. Something amazing like last time."

"Yeah, but how do we do that?" asked Brian. "How do we find an epic, incredible adventure again?"

"Maybe I could look to see what NASA's doing. There may be a clue about some kind of danger from space that we could solve," I suggested.

Brian didn't like that idea. "Even if you found out about something, how would we get NASA to even listen to us? They have no idea what we've already done. It's a total secret. They'd say we're just kids."

Brian was right, but I didn't like his attitude. "Listen, Brian. This is an Official EMU Club Meeting. Before you talk, you've got to make a motion, and it has to be seconded."

"What are you talking about? What's a motion?"

"I'm the president of the club," I reminded Brian, "and these meetings have got to have rules about who can talk and when they can talk. Otherwise, we'll have everyone talking all at once."

"First of all, there's only two of us."

"Doesn't change anything," I said.

"And second of all, you're the president, but I'm the C.E.O. It stands for chief executive officer, and that's a higher rank!"

"That's a technicality. Wait!" I said suddenly. "I've got to get a picture of this historic meeting. Future generations are going to want to see how we decided on our second adventure." Violet was at ceramics camp with her friend Emma, so I had the camera and had to be the selfie photographer.

For the record, I do not have a phone, even though I totally should. My parents gave me a camera instead, because they said they believe in "creativity." Seems to me some of the games I would play on a phone were made by some pretty creative people.

Brian took a breath. "Now can we have a normal conversation like two normal people?"

I looked at him. "Your motion is seconded. I'll allow it."

Brian moaned and rolled his eyes again. Insubordination, but I let it go. He said, "Look, we didn't find our first mystery by trying to figure out how we could save the world. We found it by trying to solve an <u>actual</u> mystery that we needed to solve: a mystery that was in our everyday lives."

I agreed. "We were just trying to find the video game controller that was lost."

"Right," continued Brian. "So our next mystery should be one that's from our real lives. One that we really just want to know the answer to."

Just then, Ferdinand ran right toward the tree next to us, barking like crazy. Probably chasing a squirrel or something. He leaped into the air, then tumbled down. He turned to look at us, panting, with his tongue hanging out.

I took a picture, then lowered the camera, shaking my head. "I'm having trouble believing Ferdinand is a genius alien robot," I said to Brian.

"Yeah, he sure acts kind of stupid most of the time."

I said, "Let's go to my room and get some ideas for what mystery we could solve."

We went inside, and of course I had to wait for Brian to wash his hands. One thing about Brian is that he washes his hands A LOT.

When we got to my room, we both sat down on the floor and wrote down possible mysteries we could solve.

We exchanged papers and looked at what we had written.

<u>Brian's ideas</u>

Mysteries

1. Is there really a Bigfoot?
2. Something about gluten allergies?

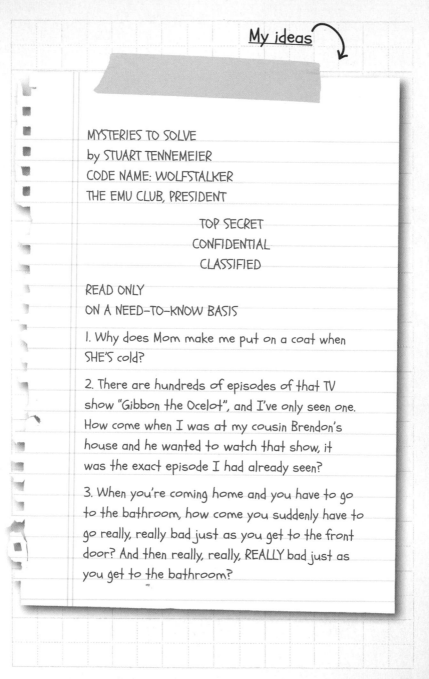

MYSTERIES TO SOLVE
by STUART TENNEMEIER
CODE NAME: WOLFSTALKER
THE EMU CLUB, PRESIDENT

TOP SECRET
CONFIDENTIAL
CLASSIFIED

READ ONLY
ON A NEED-TO-KNOW BASIS

1. Why does Mom make me put on a coat when SHE'S cold?

2. There are hundreds of episodes of that TV show "Gibbon the Ocelot", and I've only seen one. How come when I was at my cousin Brendon's house and he wanted to watch that show, it was the exact episode I had already seen?

3. When you're coming home and you have to go to the bathroom, how come you suddenly have to go really, really bad just as you get to the front door? And then really, really, REALLY bad just as you get to the bathroom?

"Okay," I said. "Mine stink. But yours are at an epic level of horribleness."

"I know," Brian replied. "I can't think of anything."

"We're going to spend time trying to solve one of these mysteries and we're either going to find a boring answer or no answer! And we're running out of time. I go back to school next week!"

Brian didn't have to go back to school because he's homeschooled and doesn't have a summer vacation. Or the whole school year is a summer vacation, I'm not sure which.

Brian said, "Well, we can still solve mysteries once school starts."

"I guess," I said. "Maybe the best one we've got is the going-to-the-bathroom one."

We heard Mom come home with my sister, Violet, and her friend Emma. Brian looked at my clock: 3:57.

"Oh," he said. "I've got to get home! I've got physics at four!"

"You can call it science, Brian. No reason to show off."

"Whatever! Mom hates it when I'm late. Let's think about that bathroom mystery," he called as he ran out of my room. He lives right next door, so he can pretty much make it home in half a minute.

I played my new <u>Block Heroes 4</u> video game in the living room until Emma left. I do <u>not</u> like to get involved with my sister and her friends. Then I went up to Violet's room. I sat down on her bed, which made me feel stupid because I was sitting next to tons of stuffed animals. A giant goofy-eyed owl was staring at me.

"Violet."

"What?"

"I just want to tell you how important it is that we keep the EMU Club a secret. You wouldn't tell Emma about it would you?"

The idea of Emma knowing about the EMU Club made me extremely nervous. Because she would tell everyone, and they would think we were liars or crazy. Or maybe someone <u>would</u> believe her, and we'd be called in by the president and Congress and the army to answer lots of questions.

But even worse, the possibility of Emma insisting on joining the club was so horrifying it made my stomach sink. Having one little kid in the club was bad enough.

"I'm not stupid, Stuart," Violet said. "I understand why we can't tell anyone."

"Okay, okay. Um . . ." I paused, not knowing how to ask this. "Um, when you came home from ceramics camp, did you have to go to the bathroom?"

"No. You want to see the mug I made?"

"No, thanks," I said, leaving the room. I'd gotten everything I could out of this conversation.

But school started the next week, and we absolutely <u>had</u> to find a mystery before school started!

OFFICIAL EMU CLUB REPORT
PART FOUR
THE PART WHERE SCHOOL STARTS AND WE STILL HAVEN'T FOUND A NEW MYSTERY

Well, no one really did any work on the going-to-the-bathroom mystery. I eventually told Violet about it, but she didn't seem too interested. Brian and I did a couple of Google searches, but we got boring answers about bladders from medical advice websites.

The mystery is kind of weird and interesting, but it's also gross. I didn't want our next adventure to be about pee.

By the morning of the first day of school, I'd pretty much given up on finding another amazing mystery. I had my new school supplies that Mom had gotten me from a list that was e-mailed to her, and I was squeezing them into my new backpack. The only mystery I was thinking about was sixth grade.

Who would be my new teacher? What would it be like in those sixth-grade classrooms? Will there be a lot more homework than in fifth grade? Will Bradley Ketchum be in my class, and will he finally leave me alone?

Bradley Ketchum is this kid who has been in my class every year since kindergarten, and is a total jerk. He got everyone to call me Beef Stew (because my name is Stu, ha-ha), and last year he once put gum in my hair as he passed me in the hall. It was so disgusting and sticky, I had to cut it out with scissors. And when my mom asked what I was doing, I had to say I wanted to give myself a haircut, which she was really mad and kind of concerned about.

So Violet and I were walking to school (we only live a couple of blocks away, and now we're allowed to walk on our own), and as we got to the school driveway, there was Bradley Ketchum with a couple of guys from my grade. I tried to walk past him without him seeing me, but he shouted out, "Hey, Baloney!" It's not my name, and I wasn't looking at him, but I still knew he was talking to me.

I should have kept walking, but I couldn't help turning back and asking, "Why did you call me Baloney?"

He shouted back at me (but he's really talking to those other guys), "Because your name is Oscar Mayer, isn't it?"

Okay, so it's a joke about my last name, Tennemeier. It sounds only a little bit like Oscar Mayer, the company that makes baloney. Ha-ha.

I tried to think of something clever to say back to Bradley Ketchum, but all I could come up with was:

"That's hilarious, Bradley." Not exactly the wittiest comeback, plus I didn't actually say it loud enough for Bradley Ketchum to hear it. I turned back to keep walking toward school. It's embarrassing enough for this to be happening in front of these guys from my grade, but in front of my little sister is pretty humiliating.

He called after me, "Save me some baloney for lunch, Baloney!" So my last name sounds only barely like a company that makes baloney—that's his big joke. The worst part was when I heard the other guys from my grade chuckle.

Once we were in school, my obligation to watch Violet was over, and two of her friends, Oliver and Amanda S., had already surrounded her, jumping up and down like monkeys, so I quickly said "Bye" and walked off toward my classroom. She said, "Bye, Stuart."

I got to my classroom and found a prime seat in the back. I always like to sit in the back so that I can work on Official Reports like this one, or make up games, or draw monsters, without the teachers noticing. As I waited for class to start, I noticed that Charlie Owens was in my class this year, which was good news. Charlie is an okay guy: he can say the alphabet backward really fast, he taught me how to turn a pen into a spitball launcher, and he has tons of "Porcupine-Person" comic books. I made a mental note to sit with him at lunch.

And then in walked Bradley Ketchum. Ugh. There were two sixth-grade classes, so he just as likely could have been in the other one, but no, he had to be in mine.

Class started, and Ms. Hansauer, my new teacher, started talking. I didn't know what I was so worried about. In my seventh year at this elementary school (middle school in my town doesn't start until seventh grade), there were no surprises. Ms. Hansauer was just another teacher. (Although she did use nasal spray a lot! Every few minutes she would put this little plastic bottle up to each nostril and squeeze a spray in.)

Anyway, after some boring talk about math and English, and a Spanish teacher coming in, it was finally lunchtime. I grabbed my brown bag lunch and headed with the rest of the class for to the cafeteria.

OFFICIAL EMU CLUB REPORT
PART FIVE
THE PART WHERE I MIGHT HAVE FOUND OUR MYSTERY (SEE IF YOU CAN SPOT IT)

So when I got to the lunchroom, I saw Charlie sitting at a table with Mark Siegel and Jason Hernandez (who are both sort of okay), and I started walking over. "Hey, Charlie, how was your summer?"

Charlie looked up and before he could finish saying, "Okay, Stuart. How was yours?," Bradley Ketchum scooted in and sat right next to Charlie.

"Hey, BALONEY. What kind of meat do you have for lunch?" Bradley Ketchum said loudly enough for several tables to hear. Did he spend the whole summer thinking up this comedy bit? He seemed awfully proud of how funny he thought it was.

A few kids laughed, and I muttered, "Pretty good," to Charlie as I passed, because there was no way I was sitting at this table now. I ended up sitting with Adam Peterson, Cam Parker, and Alison Parsons, who are called the "P Triplets" because their last names all start with "P" and they've been best, best friends since kindergarten, and all they talked about was this robotics camp they went to during the last two weeks of vacation.

(For the record, my lunch was not baloney. It was a peanut butter sandwich.)

After getting picked fourth to last for touch football teams at recess, it was officially a Pretty Bad First Day of Sixth Grade.

I made it through the rest of the day, and then settled into the last period, social studies, waiting for this day to finally be over.

School ended at 3:10, but waiting for that to come took forever! From 2:40 on, it seemed like the second hand on the clock on the wall was going so SLLLLOOOOWWWWWWWLLLLYYYY, I couldn't stand it. Ms. Hansauer kept talking and talking and . . .

FINALLY, the bell rang and it was 3:10 and I could go home. I didn't have to walk Violet home because she was getting picked up by my mom, who was taking her to after-school soccer.

I walked past Brian's house, and sure enough, there he was on his front porch, reading. He didn't have a horrible day with Bradley Ketchum, and he didn't play an entire game of touch football at recess without getting a single ball thrown to him, and he didn't have to sit through boring Ms. Hansauer as she shot nasal spray into her nostrils, and the water fountain didn't splash on him so that it looked like he had peed in his pants. He had a day of homeschooling, and hanging out on the computer, maybe doing some workbooks.

I walked up onto the porch and sat down next to him. I guess he could tell what kind of day I had had by the way I sat down, because he said, "Sixth grade pretty rough, huh?"

"Ah, it's not so different than fifth grade. There's just more of it. You are so lucky you don't have to go."

"I'm not sure about that," Brian replied. "What are you studying this year?"

"I don't know. I think we're starting with the Civil War in social studies. It's hard to know because it's so boring I can't even pay attention."

"The Civil War is really cool," Brian said.

"Maybe," I said, "but our class on it today went on and on and on. It was like time slowed down and 3:10 was never going to come."

I got up. I said to Brian, "I'd better get home." I didn't have any homework, but I was exhausted.

OFFICIAL EMU CLUB REPORT

PART SIX

IS THIS THE END OF THE EMU CLUB????

No, it's not.

But it sort of felt like it. Violet was doing her third-grade stuff, and Brian was busy preparing for a didgeridoo concert in Akron, and I was slogging through sixth grade.

We had no mystery and we had no club.

I just felt like the EMU Club was over.

And then on a Friday night, Brian was sleeping over (because his mom had a meeting or something), and we were hanging out watching TV.

"How's social studies going?" Brian asked.

"It's okay," I said. "Just spelunking boring."

I'm trying to get the word "spelunking" to catch on and become a word that means "totally" or "very." I figure if I use it, my friends will start using it, and then their friends, and soon the whole country and the whole world will be saying "spelunking." So far, it's not working.

Brian said, "Something you said on the first day of school got me thinking. You said it felt like time goes slowly right before school ends."

"Yeah! It's crazy. Every day, it feels like it takes forever to get from 2:40 to 3:10."

Brian said, "Well, why does that happen? Why does time go slowly in certain places, at certain times?"

I never thought of asking why. "I don't know." But I knew what Brian was thinking. "Maybe that's our next mystery."

"Yes!" Brian said.

We went into Violet's room, where she was reading some book about wizards and magic.

I explained the mystery to Violet. She said, "That is weird. Sometimes time <u>does</u> go really fast, and sometimes <u>really</u> slowly. It takes twenty minutes to watch a 'See Ya, Wouldn't Want to Be Ya'"—that's Violet's favorite TV show—"and it takes twenty minutes to drive to Grandma's house, but it seems like the TV show is <u>a lot</u> shorter."

"Yeah," I agreed, "that's true. And you would not believe how slowly social studies goes, especially right when school's about to end."

Violet asked, "How are we going to investigate that?"

Brian said, "Yeah, it's not like we can go to your classroom with a magnifying glass and find clues."

I said, "Well, tomorrow's Saturday and it's the book fair at school. What if we go, and then sneak away to look at the classroom, to see what we can find?"

I could see Brian was having second thoughts. He said, "Okay, but . . . this may be one of those mysteries where there's really no answer. Or a boring answer."

I thought, "Maybe so, but at least the EMU Club is back in business!"

PART SEVEN

THE PART WHERE SOMETHING SCARY HAPPENS (OKAY, NOT SUPER SCARY. THE SUPER-SCARY STUFF COMES LATER. BUT I WAS PLENTY SCARED)

On Saturday morning, Violet woke us up by taking this picture. She was surprisingly excited about the day's investigation at school.

We had breakfast—banana pancakes for Violet, plain pancakes for me (bananas are slimy and gross), and rice cakes for Brian (he's not allowed to have pancakes)—and told my parents we wanted to spend the day at the book fair. Mom insisted on coming even though we totally walk to school by ourselves. She and Dad gave us each $15 for books (including Brian!). SCORE!

We walked to school and wandered around the book fair, which was in the gym. We had a mystery to solve, but why not get some books while we were undercover? I found this awesome book about the most disgusting animals in the world. Did you know there's a hairy frog that lives in Africa that breaks its own bones to use as weapons when it's attacked? So cool.

Anyway, after a while, Mom got into a conversation with a couple of other moms and Ms. Jackson, my second-grade teacher who I'd often see smoking in her car and who always smelled like peppermint. Brian, Violet, and I convened, and I whispered, "Mom's distracted. Let's make our move. Walk CASUALLY out of the gym."

Violet said, "What's CASUALLY?"

"Like it's no big deal, like nothing's up," I told her.

The three of us walked toward the gym exit as naturally as we could, as though nothing was going on, and we weren't going to launch an investigation in a classroom, where we weren't allowed. I sort of whistled as I walked past tables of books, to show how carefree I was (but I can't really whistle, so it just sort of sounded like blowing).

In the hallway outside the gym, I laid out the plan. "Okay," I whispered. "We're fine here because this is where anyone would go if they were going to the bathroom. But once we pass the bathrooms down the hall, we can't use that excuse."

"Right," Brian said, and started walking down the hall.

"Wait!" I hissed. "If you see anyone who could spot us, make a bird call sound. Like this: CAW! CAW!"

"That's the dumbest thing I've ever heard," Brian said. "Even if we could make it sound like a real bird, that would be even <u>more</u> suspicious than three kids walking down the hall of a school! Why would a bird be in the school?"

Brian didn't know very much about how to do an investigation. "That's the way it's done, Brian. You can't just say, 'Hold it! I think someone may see us!'"

Brian began to respond, "Yes, it . . ." when we heard down the hall:

"Guys!"

Violet had already walked down the hall toward the stairs and had passed the bathrooms.

Brian and I ran to catch up. I was working with amateurs!

Upstairs is where the grades four through six classrooms are. It was weird to see this hallway, which is usually brightly lit and full of bustling kids, so dark and empty. I led the way toward my classroom; the only sound was the occasional sneaker squeak on the floor.

We got to my classroom, and I put my hand on the doorknob. LOCKED!

I turned to Violet and Brian. "I didn't know they locked the classrooms on weekends!" I whispered.

We walked silently back down the hall to the stairway, and just as we got there, I heard a noise, like a door opening.

I turned and looked back down the hall and saw the door to Room 4B open! And coming out was the school janitor!

We scurried into the stairway. I saved the Earth from an alien invasion (see: First Official Report of the EMU Club), but my heart had never beat faster than it did when we barely made it out of sight in time.

I peeked around the corner to see the janitor, sort of a weird-looking guy—tall, with long hair, and one of those mustache-beards that just goes around the mouth but not on the cheeks—pushing his cart out of 4B.

I figured I'd get a picture of the hallway for our records. "Give me the camera," I whispered to

Violet. She handed it to me, and I held it out past the corner, pointing down the hall, and took this picture.

"Let's get out of here," Violet said.

OFFICIAL EMU CLUB REPORT

PART EIGHT

THE PART WHERE WE ACTUALLY, FINALLY GET . . . A CLUE!! BUT MORE IMPORTANT, THE CREEPIEST THING <u>EVER</u> HAPPENS

We went home with Mom and got lunch. (Tomato soup and grilled cheese for Violet and Brian; just grilled cheese for me. Tomato soup is one of the worst foods ever invented. It's just hot red gunk!) Then we convinced Mom to let the three of us walk back to school alone.

She was surprised we wanted to go back to the book fair, but we convinced her we just loved books. I think it was my line, "I'm thirsting for knowledge!" that got her.

Back at the book fair, we got ready for another try at the classroom. "Maybe this time the door will be unlocked," Brian said hopefully.

After Brian washed his hands in the boys' room, we made our way back up to the grades four through six hallway. I peeked in from the stairs. The coast was clear.

We VERY quietly and VERY carefully tiptoed back to my classroom. I put my hand on the doorknob. It turned, and the door opened!

We jumped inside and closed the door as quietly as we could. "Whew," I said. "The janitor must have cleaned in here and forgot to re-lock the door."

I looked around. It's super weird to be in your classroom without the class or teacher there. Dark, quiet, and eerie.

"Where do you sit?" Brian asked. I showed him my seat in the back.

Violet was looking all around. It's kind of a thrill to be in the sixth-grade classroom when you're in third grade.

I sat in my seat, and Brian sat in the seat next to mine, Angela Montgomery's seat. I didn't tell Brian that Angela bites her nails and wipes them on her seat.

Brian and I looked at the clock: 2:14. We watched the clock for a minute: 2:15.

"That did seem like a long minute," Brian said.

"What did I tell you?" I smiled.

"Didn't seem so long," Violet said, as she looked at the Family History projects on the wall up by the teacher's desk.

"Violet, believe me, it was," I said to her. What does she know about time? She didn't even know what a minute was a few years ago.

"Let's try it again," Brian said.

We watched the clock.

2:16.

2:17.

"Okay, that felt like, probably a minute and a half! Maybe TWO minutes!" I said.

"I don't think so," Violet said.

"Whatever," I said. Clearly we were going to get further if we ignored her.

"Wait," Brian said. "Let's switch places."

"Okay." So Brian and I stood in the front of the room, and Violet sat in my seat."

2:18.

2:19.

"You know," I admitted, "That didn't seem quite so long."

"Yeah," said Brian, his hands in the air, like he was trying to _feel_ time.

"It was crazy long!" Violet said from the back of the room. "That was the longest minute of my life."

Wow.

We experimented by positioning ourselves all around the room, and sure enough, the closer to the back of the room, the slower time got. And from about 2:30 to 3:00, it got even slower.

"This is wild," I said. "But what could cause this? What do we do now?"

Brian offered, "Should we go home and see what we can find out on Google?"

Violet said, "Maybe there's a book on this at the book fair!"

Brian sat down in Amy Horowitz's seat. "Stuart," he began.

"WolfStalker," I reminded him. We were on a case, after all.

"WolfStalker," Brian continued, looking toward the back wall of the classroom. "What's the room next to this one, behind that back wall?"

"Room 6A. No, wait, there's something between the two rooms. The . . . maintenance closet."

Brian stood up. "We've got to check it out."

First we went into the hallway and peeked into every classroom. No janitor.

Then we looked at the maintenance closet. I lay down on the floor to look under the door to see if there was a light on. It looked dark.

I was about to reach for the doorknob when I got an idea. "Brian, you should open the door," I whispered. "If the janitor's in there, you can't get in trouble; you don't go to this school!"

Brian didn't like my logic, but he couldn't disagree with it. Violet and I waited by the stairs so we could make a getaway if there was a problem, and watched Brian down the hall at the closet door.

It opened. Brian went in, we saw a light go on, and then he poked his head back out to wave us over. Whew.

The closet was pretty small, with lots of shelves of cleaning supplies. We looked all around but couldn't find anything unusual.

"Let's try it," whispered Brian. He held out his wristwatch, and we all huddled around it.

3:11.

I got really bored, and started thinking about Scottish accents and I wondered if Scottish people <u>thought</u> in Scottish accents inside their heads, and how weird that would be to <u>think</u> with that strange accent that almost sounds like singing, and wouldn't that be distracting when, say, you're trying to do a math problem and . . .

3:12.

"Whoa! That was a LONG minute!!" I tried to whisper but it got a bit too loud.

Brian and Violet both nodded in agreement, eyes wide.

Brian said, "I thought that maybe if time goes slower in the back of the room, it could go even slower in the room behind it."

We looked around for ANY clue. Brian looked under containers of soap and stuff. Violet looked in the back of the shelves. It was kind of hard because there wasn't that much room for the three of us to move around in. Violet found a gum wrapper. Brian thought it was weird the way the light flickered a little bit. I saw a small calendar on the wall with the month of September and a picture of a lake on it. Every day was crossed out up to that day's date.

Then Brian coughed. "Shh!" I warned him.

"I can't help it," Brian whispered back. "It's dusty in here. Or I'm allergic to some of this cleaning stuff."

Brian is allergic to tons of stuff. It may be one of the reasons he's crazy about washing his hands all the time. But I doubt it.

Brian coughed again, and we decided to leave the closet before we got caught.

As we walked down the hall toward the stairs, I began to say something about the gum wrapper, when we heard a noise behind us.

We whirled around, and the door to the maintenance closet opened. And the janitor came out.

He looked at us. Not angry, like, <u>You kids aren't allowed to be in these halls on a Saturday!</u> More like, <u>Huh?</u> He just stood there and looked at us.

And we froze and looked back at him.

Talk about time slowing down. It seemed like it stood as still as we were.

And then we ran.

We ran down the stairs as fast as we could, and down the hall past the bathrooms and into the gym and we didn't stop until we were safely among all the kids and parents shopping and talking.

"Where did he . . ." I started.

"How did he . . ." Brian started.

"We were just in that closet!! How could he come out of it right after us?" Violet whisper-screamed.

"Could he have been in there with us?" I asked.

"Not a chance!" Brian said, which was obvious. "It's just a small closet, and there's no place to hide!"

"Could he have slipped in after us, and then turned around and come out?" I asked, knowing full well what the answer was.

"No way!" Violet said.

"We'd just left the closet a couple of seconds before he came out!" Brian agreed.

I said, "Something absolutely bizarrely creepy is going on, and it all centers around that janitor."

Violet said, "And he saw us!"

OFFICIAL EMU CLUB REPORT
PART NINE
THE PART WHERE I FIND OUT WHO ... OR WHAT ... THE JANITOR IS

If I felt uncomfortable going to school when the scariest thing was Bradley Ketchum calling me Baloney, imagine how I felt going when I knew that <u>janitor</u> was going to be there!

In the days after the book fair, Violet and I decided to try to watch the janitor to get clues, but he was watching us, too. Well, I'm not so sure he was watching me, but Violet said every time she saw him in the halls, she'd try to act natural and casually keep walking (now that she knew the word "casual," she liked to use it all the time), but she could tell he was <u>staring</u> at her.

I did find out that his name is Mr. Hartoonian, and he's new this year. He replaced the old janitor, Mr. O'Neill, who left the school after last year. Mr. O'Neill was a really nice guy who called all the kids Mr. and Ms. as a joke. "Mr. Tennemeier!" he'd say to me in the morning.

Mr. Hartoonian didn't really talk to the kids. He kept to himself, but the few times I heard him talk, usually to a teacher or Ms. Penscher (the principal of the school), he talked kind of weird. I don't know what kind of accent he had, but he was definitely not from America.

The three of us tried to figure out some explanation for the time-slowing and the janitor-appearing-out-of-nowhere, but we could not.

We knew we needed to find out more about Mr. Hartoonian, and his closet, but I was definitely nervous about the idea of spying on someone like that. The guy was definitely spooky.

Weeks went by, and I found out nothing new about Mr. Hartoonian.

Meanwhile, Bradley Ketchum kept calling me Baloney, and soon other people were calling me Baloney, too. First it was just Gregg and Myron, Bradley Ketchum's two best buddies. But then other kids starting doing it.

Once even Charlie Owens called me Baloney, but he didn't do it to be mean; he just slipped. He quickly said, "Oh, sorry, Stuart."

The worst was when the boys ran a race in P.E. and I came in last (I got a cramp in my side, and I hadn't gotten enough sleep the night before, plus the sun got in my eyes just as we started). Bradley Ketchum was waiting at the finish line, saying, "Hey, Oscar Mayer! You're full of baloney!" Which doesn't even make sense because "full of baloney" means you're a liar, not a slow runner.

Speaking of slow, social studies continued to go as slowly as ever. I tried to move to the front of the class (even being close to Ms. Hansauer would be worth having time move normally in the afternoons) but no one would trade with me.

So one day, I was sitting in the back, DYING from slow-time-movement while Ms. Hansauer was yakking about Reconstruction, and I flipped through the pages of our social studies textbook. I decided to look ahead to World War II to see if I could find any cool war pictures.

I was looking at the pages, bored out of my skull, when I saw something that made me actually gasp. Like, OUT LOUD! Kids turned around to look at me, but I covered my mouth and continued staring, wide eyed, at this picture.

Here is Franklin D. Roosevelt in 1899, when he was only 17 years old. He grew up in Hyde Park, New York.

...came Governor

...bitions

(I took this picture of the page later.)

This is a picture of a young Franklin Roosevelt, who would grow up to become the president of the United States during World War II. And the guy standing behind him, next to the tree is . . . Mr. Hartoonian.

This picture was taken in 1899!

And Mr. Hartoonian looks the same as he does today!

I looked up, and while Ms. Hansauer spoke, a few kids around me were still turned around in their chairs, staring at me. My mouth was hanging open behind my hands, my eyes were wide, and my expression looked like I had just seen . . .

A GHOST.

OFFICIAL EMU CLUB REPORT

PART TEN

THE PART WITH THE HALLOWEEN PARTY. AND THE PART WHERE MR. HARTOONIAN TALKS TO US, AND IT IS SPELUNKING <u>SPOOKY</u>!

That afternoon, Brian, Violet, and I huddled around my social studies book in my room and just LOOKED at it.

"You think Mr. Hartoonian is a ghost?" Brian said.

"Yes! He must have lived years and years ago, when this picture was taken, then died, and now he looks exactly the same because he's a ghost! He's in my social studies book, Brian!"

Violet said, "Maybe he was a ghost when this picture was taken."

"Maybe," I said. "But I don't think you can take a picture of a ghost."

"I think that's vampires," Brian said.

"WHAT IF HE'S A VAMPIRE!!" I said. The thought of a bloodsucking vampire at my school who suspects I'm spying on him sent a chill down my spine.

Brian said, "He can't be a vampire. They only come out at night. Sunlight burns their skin."

Of course I knew this. I just got suddenly startled by the thought.

"Then he's a ghost. This totally fits!" I said to Brian. "Ghosts can appear and disappear, and they can walk through walls. That explains how he came out of the maintenance closet after we did!"

"I think you're right," Violet said. This means I <u>had</u> to be right. Violet never agrees with me. It's one of her principles of living.

"But what does a ghost have to do with time slowing down?" Brian asked.

"How should I know?" Brian was clearly getting bogged down by details, when there was an ACTUAL GHOST IN MY SCHOOL. "We don't know everything about ghosts. Maybe time-slowing is one of their powers. Maybe for some reason that's the way he's chosen to haunt our school: by stealing the passage of time!"

"Okay, okay," Brian said. "This is a huge clue, and your ghost theory is good. I didn't believe in ghosts, but I didn't believe in aliens until we fought them last summer. What do we do now?"

"We need to learn about ghosts!" Violet said. "How do you get rid of them?"

"Right. Silver bullets?" I asked.

"Silver bullets kill werewolves, not ghosts," Brian said. He really knew his monsters.

Whatever! I quickly added, "We also need to find out why he's haunting our school!"

"Okay," Brian said. "I'll find out ghost information, and I'll also look up the history of the school to see if I can find out why he'd be haunting it. But we've got to get back into his closet."

"Are you nuts?!" I shouted. "I'm not going back in there. What if he suddenly appears?"

"It's the only place we can look for more clues, now that we know what Mr. Hartoonian is," Brian explained.

"We? Who's 'we'? I'm the only one who can do it because the closet is next to my classroom. Violet's classroom is in another part of the school, and you don't even go to the school. I'm going to be the one who has to walk into a haunted closet!"

Well, it turned out I couldn't, because over the next few weeks, every time I got up the courage to ask to go to the bathroom and then try to open the maintenance closet door when no one was watching, the door was locked.

And each time it was locked and I couldn't go in, I was totally relieved.

I realized the only time Mr. Hartoonian gets careless and leaves the closet door unlocked is when there's no school going on, like on Saturdays, because he doesn't expect kids to be around.

So I came up with a plan. The next time we could be at school on a Saturday would be the weekend before Halloween. My school always has a Halloween party, and kids can come in costume, and the kindergarteners have a parade, and there's games and stuff. Just like at the book fair, Brian can come to the party, and we can sneak out and head over to the closet.

Here is just the first page of the plan I made for the Halloween party:

The main thing was that Violet would find Mr. Hartoonian and keep an eye on him while Brian and I went to the closet. If Mr. Hartoonian started going back to the closet, or disappeared, or flew away or something, she would warn us with a birdcall.

And the Halloween party was perfect for our plan. Brian and I could dress as ninjas, so no one would think it's strange that we're wearing all black, and we could blend into the shadows. Violet could wear my "Creature from the Black Lagoon" mask because it will cover her whole face. Mr. Hartoonian won't recognize her, and she can follow him around without him noticing.

The afternoon of the party, Brian came over to my house.

He came into my room in his ninja costume as Violet and I were finishing putting on our costumes. "What do you think?" he asked.

I looked at him. "Um, how about a salute?"

"What?"

I explained, "When you approach a superior officer, you're supposed to <u>salute</u>."

"Will you cut that out? Let's get going." Brian waved me off.

"It's a sign of respect. I did write up that awesome plan. Did you memorize it?"

"What we're going to do is really pretty simple. You didn't have to make it so complicated," Brian said.

"That doesn't answer the question," I told Brian.

"I'm taking it with me. I can't remember all these birdcalls," Violet said.

"You can't take it with you, Violet! If you get caught, they'll see the plan and know <u>everything</u>! I told you, you have to memorize it!"

Violet said, "I'll just go, 'CAW, CAW!' if he's coming. I don't really get it, anyway. By the time you hear me, it will be too late for you to get out of there."

Next, Brian started challenging my plan. "Well, why do I have to take this list of hand signals? I've memorized it."

I was getting impatient. These people knew nothing about creating a good plan for investigating. "Because I made it small enough that if we get caught, you can eat it."

"I'm not eating this piece of paper!" Brian said.

"Only if we're caught!" I explained. It's not like I made it for him to eat!

"Forget it," Brian said. "Can we just go to the party? If we wait too long, we'll run out of time."

Because we promised to be back before it started getting dark, Mom and Dad let us go to the Halloween party by ourselves, as long as Brian and I stuck with Violet as we crossed the two streets, especially Elm.

First thing we did at the party was find the pigs in a blanket, because those are awesome. I had, like, twenty.

Then I whispered to Brian and Violet, "Operation Jackal Fire is a go."

"What?" Violet said.

"Operation Jackal Fire is a go."

"What's a Jeckle Fire?" Violet asked, too loudly.

"It's the name of what we're doing! Didn't you read page five of the plan?"

"Let's just go," Brian said.

We looked all around the gym to be sure Mr. Hartoonian wasn't in there. Violet kept seeing friends who wanted her to join them, but she knew to keep close to us.

We were about to leave the gym to look for Mr. Hartoonian around the rest of the school, when I heard behind me, "Hey, Baloney!"

I turned around and there was Bradley Ketchum. He wasn't even wearing a costume. He had come to the party with a bunch of sixth graders, but luckily they hadn't followed him over to watch him harass me.

Bradley Ketchum looked at Brian and said to me, "Ninja Oscar Mayer, who's this? Your friend Ninja Ronald McDonald?"

Brian took off his hood. "You know me, Bradley. I'm Brian Hrznicz. I went to this school for kindergarten and first grade." Brian is a smart guy, but he could be totally clueless about certain things. Bradley hadn't come over here to have a kindergarten reunion.

"Oh, yeah. Brian. You hang out with Baloney here?"

Before Brian could explain to Bradley Ketchum what my actual name is, I said, "We've got to go," and we left the gym.

We walked around the downstairs hallway sort of pretending to look for the bathroom, and eventually looked into Room 2A and saw Mr. Hartoonian with a mop.

We shot our heads away from the window in the door. "Do you think he saw us?" I asked.

"I don't think so," Brian said.

I waved two fingers next to my head.

"What's that?" Violet asked.

"It means we're going to go."

I pointed at Violet and then waved my hand across.

"What does that mean?" Violet asked.

I said, "There's no point in my doing these hand signals if we say what they mean each time!!"

Brian said to Violet, "It means you stay here. Try to watch Mr. Hartoonian without being noticed.

You know what to do if he comes toward the maintenance closet."

I gave Brian the two-finger wave next to my head again, but this time I kind of yelled it at him with my eyes.

"Okay, okay."

We walked up the stairs, and then we were in the dark, quiet grades four through six hallway. We walked to the maintenance closet door. It felt much better being there, knowing that Violet was keeping an eye on Mr. Hartoonian.

Unless he pulls some kind of ghost trick and suddenly appears here! My stomach sank.

I put my hand on the doorknob. It turned. Unlocked!

Brian and I crept in, turned the light on, and closed the door. I could tell Brian was scared, so I said, "Let's hurry!" We looked frantically around for clues.

It did occur to me that we had one advantage: because of the time-slowing thing, we had lots of time. We could do a pretty big search and maybe a minute would go by.

Then Brian coughed. So much for that advantage.

I looked at the little calendar on the wall. Now it was on the October page (with a picture of the mountain in the fall), and all the days up to that day were crossed out.

I turned the page. The November dates were blank, except the first Tuesday was circled. And under the circle were the words "How to Destroy."

"Brian!" I whispered.

He put down a bucket and looked, trying not to cough. We looked at each other, and then he paged through the rest of the calendar. It went all the way through next year, but nothing else was circled or crossed off or written on it. Just that first Tuesday in November.

And then we heard, from far away outside the closet, the worst sound I could ever imagine hearing:

"CAW, CAW! CAW, CAW!"

It was Violet, signaling us. Mr. Hartoonian was coming!

Brian and I got so scared we bumped into each other.

"CAW, CAW!"

Brian reached for the closet door, and I reached to turn out the light.

"CAW, CAW!"

The door opened, and because I had reached across Brian for the light switch, he bumped into my arm, and then I tripped, and we both spilled out of the closet and fell onto the hallway floor.

"Caw . . . caw?"

We looked up from the floor and saw Bradley Ketchum walking toward us, Violet walking behind him.

"What are you guys DOING?" he yelled.

My plan had several options for things we could say if we were caught, but they were written with the idea we might get caught by a teacher or Ms. Penscher, the principal. Not Bradley Ketchum. I chose one anyway.

"Brian spilled some chocolate milk, and we came here to get cleaning supplies," I said from the floor.

"You guys are so weird," Bradley Ketchum said.

Brian and I got up. "No, we're not," was all I could think of to say.

Suddenly Violet said, "Come on, let's get out of here!" And it seemed to all four of us like that was a good idea. We ran for the stairs.

I led the way, and just as I turned the corner to run down the stairs, BAM!

I hit something.

I fell down, and then the other kids did.

Once again, I looked up from the floor, but this time I saw . . . Mr. Hartoonian.

"What's are going on? You kids not supposed to being up here."

Unless a ghost has ever talked to you, you'd have no idea how spooky it is. All four of us barely even stood back up, but just about fell down the stairs until we could regain our footing and then ran the rest of the way.

It wasn't until we were back in the gym that I could bear to turn around and see if Mr. Hartoonian was chasing us.

He wasn't.

Bradley Ketchum said, "You weirdos! We almost got caught!" He had no idea WHAT almost caught us.

Brian, Violet, and I didn't say anything to Bradley Ketchum. In fact, we walked right through the party and out of the school, and walked home without a sound, except for a few coughs from Brian.

As we walked through the cold, late afternoon, the wind blowing yellow and red leaves across the sidewalk, weirder and weirder thoughts ran through my mind.

A ghost can be invisible. Mr. Hartoonian could be right here with us. He could be in my home. In my room, while I slept!

OFFICIAL EMU CLUB REPORT
PART ELEVEN
THE PART WHERE WE PREPARE FOR BATTLE WITH A GHOST

Back at my house, Violet explained that she saw Bradley Ketchum watch us go up the stairs, and then follow us. And she thought even though she was supposed to watch Mr. Hartoonian, she'd better run upstairs and warn us that Bradley Ketchum was coming.

The whole thing seemed like a disaster, but it also seemed to me we'd gotten what we wanted: another clue. "So," I said to Brian and Violet in my room, "what happens on that Tuesday in November?"

"How could we know?" asked Violet.

"It could be nothing," I said. "Maybe the day he gets his pants back from the ghost cleaners."

"But the note said 'How to Destroy,'" Brian said. "He's planning something really bad."

"Why is he haunting our school?!" Violet asked.

Brian said, "I looked up the history of the school and couldn't find any reason a ghost would want to haunt it."

"For a ghost with no reason to haunt a school, he's sure doing a good job of it," I said.

"Maybe we should just ask him," Brian said.

"You don't just walk up to a ghost and ask him why he's doing his haunting!" The less contact I had with Mr. Hartoonian, the better.

Brian said, "Well, we should at least find out what happens on that Tuesday."

"We have that day off from school," I said. A guy like me keeps very careful track of school vacation days. "But if he's planning something when he wants no one around, there are lots of days with no school, including weekends."

Brian's eyes widened, like he had just thought of something. "But why is there no school on that day?"

"I don't know. When we get a day off from school, I don't ask any questions. I just take it."

"It's Election Day!" Brian said. "There's no school because they use the school for people in town to vote in."

That was definitely interesting. "So a ghost gets a job in a school, and then circles only one date on his calendar: the date he's waiting for, the reason he's there."

Brian said, "The day he's going to find out 'How to Destroy.'"

Violet said, "He's going to haunt the school while all the grown-ups vote there?"

"Or do <u>something</u> ghostly," I said. "Who knows what!"

Brian said, "It's got to be something really bad. We've got to stop him."

We spent the next few days getting ready for the big day.

I had a theory that if Mr. Hartoonian became invisible, he'd become sort of like a vapor, or smoke, so we'd know he was around if I had a smoke detector. Smoke detectors are supposed to be stuck up on your wall so that if there's a fire, the smoke would set off the alarm and everybody in the house would wake up. We had an extra one in the garage, and I attached it to one of Dad's golf clubs, and I made . . . a GHOST DETECTOR™.

That ™ means that it's my invention, and nobody can steal my idea.

Brian did some computer research on ghosts, and had a theory of his own. "I wouldn't have thought ghosts were real. But if there are ghosts, there must be some scientific explanation. So I think ionized . . ." Blah, blah, blah. The bottom line was that Brian got something called a Tesla ionizer and hooked it up to a battery in his backpack. He had a theory that it would defeat a ghost, and Ferdinand, my robot dog, who happens to be a technical genius, helped him build it. (Except when Brian went to Akron for his didgeridoo concert, Ferdinand basically finished it for him.)

Violet said that Mr. Hartoonian seemed solid, but because he was a ghost, she should be able to suck him up into a Dustbuster, one of those miniature vacuum cleaners. She also said something about Mr. Hartoonian moving the air pressure to travel, but I was pretty sure she just got that idea from a movie, so I stopped listening.

Okay, this Dustbuster idea seemed pretty lame, but when you thought about it, so did the ionizer and Ghost Detector™. Who knows <u>what</u> will work against a ghost?

In fact, when I thought about it, it seemed like there was no way three kids were going to stop a ghost from doing whatever horrible thing it wanted to do.

PART TWELVE

THE PART WHERE WE ABSOLUTELY, TOTALLY, NO-DOUBT-ABOUT-IT DEFEAT A GHOST

Tuesday morning.

Voting opened super early, at 7:30 a.m., so we all got ready at 7:00. We had begged my parents to let us go to school for Election Day, and I was surprised when they let us. I think they were happy with the way we were handling our independence.

We packed up our ghost-fighting stuff, and I also stocked my backpack with notebooks, pens, and my hand signal charts.

"We don't really have a plan!" Brian said, as we walked.

"We've got all this stuff. We'll just have to look at the situation when we get there, and then figure it out," I told him.

"Mr. Hartoonian wants to destroy something. Whatever it is, we've got to stop him," Violet said.

When we arrived at the school, there was only one car in the parking lot. We were sure it was Mr. Hartoonian's.

The front door was locked, but we climbed in through a window to a third-grade classroom. The window was left unlocked; ghosts make terrible janitors.

We walked as quietly as we could out of the classroom and into the hallway. I was holding out my Ghost Detector™ in front of me so Mr. Hartoonian couldn't sneak up on us.

We walked past the gym, with all the voting machines lined up and ready to go.

CRASH.

Well, maybe not a loud CRASH, but we heard something down the hall from the gym. The sound came from the hallway near the nurse's office. Around the corner was the sports supplies closet. This was the closet where all the balls and gymnastics equipment and volleyball nets and stuff were kept. It's kind of inconvenient because it's not that close to the gym.

But that must have been where the sound came from.

We looked at one another.

I made the decision that Brian should go first, in case it was a trap, and if we were attacked from the rear, I'd be in a better position to defend us.

We silently tiptoed down the hall.

We got to the corner, Violet got the camera ready, we all took a deep breath, and then jumped out.

Mr. Hartoonian was standing there with a baseball bat, looking absolutely shocked to see us! What was Mr. Hartoonian doing at the sports supplies closet? We had no idea, but I knew there was only one thing to do:

Push him back into the closet.

Mr. Hartoonian was so shocked to see us, he dropped the bat and stuff he was holding and slipped backward on a jump rope, so it was surprisingly easy for me to push him into the closet, and then slam the door closed.

Brian and I moved like we had practiced this all before. He grabbed the jump rope from the floor and began wrapping it around the doorknob, and I slid the bench outside the nurse's office over to the door. In about half a second, we had the ghost trapped in the closet.

Ghost? We trapped a GHOST in the closet?

Why couldn't he just spook his way out?

Mr. Hartoonian was pounding on the door, yelling, "Letting me out!! What are you kids to doing??"

We looked at each other. What _had_ we done?

Brian, out of breath, panted, "How did we . . . ? How could he . . . ?"

I just panted back, "I don't know!!"

"What's THAT?" Violet said, pointing to the ground.

It looked like some kind of small metallic toy animal, and it was flopping around, moving toward the closet, like it was ALIVE!

"It's trying to let him out!" Brian yelled.

Then little metal legs began growing out from its sides, and it began walking toward the closet like a bug!

That was about the scariest thing imaginable. The idea that not only was this creepy thing alive, but that it knew what was going on, and could GROW LEGS and was going to let Mr. Hartoonian out of the closet . . .

I SMASHED it with the baseball bat.

It lay there, broken. All we could hear was Mr. Hartoonian.

"What happened?? What is the going on?? Letting me out!!"

But then we could hear high-heeled footsteps coming down the hall.

We dropped all our stuff, took off our backpacks, and ran around the corner to see . . . Ms. Penscher, the principal.

"What on earth are you kids doing here?"

I had to think fast. "We came to watch the voting, Ms. Penscher."

"You want to watch voting?" she repeated, looking at me like she was trying to decide whether to believe me or not.

Luckily, we were around the corner from the sports supplies closet, so we could not hear Mr. Hartoonian screaming.

"Sure! I'm a big fan of democracy. I thought it would be cool to use my day off to observe it in action."

"Observe it in action?" Ms. Penscher repeated. She was so puzzled by what I was saying, all she could do was repeat what I said.

"Yes!" I tried to sound sincere and enthusiastic.

"We're just getting started," Ms. Penscher said. "Who let you in?"

I was not going to say that we had climbed in the third-grade window. I heard myself say brightly, "Mr. Hartoonian let us in."

That seemed to shake Ms. Penscher out of her confusion, and suddenly she was very interested. "Well, he shouldn't have. But he's here? I couldn't find him."

"Yup," I said.

She was clearly distracted by the fact that she couldn't find Mr. Hartoonian. But then we got even luckier.

One of the election workers approached us. "Excuse me, Ms. Penscher," said the older lady.

"We can't find the thermostat, and some people are complaining that it's too cold."

Ms. Penscher said, "I simply do not know where the janitor is. I'm so sorry. Here, I'll show you."

And the two of them hurried off.

Whew.

We could see the other election workers getting set up in the gym beyond the hallway. We huddled together.

"Okay," Brian said. "You can't hear Mr. Hartoonian at this end of this hallway."

"Then we have to make sure no one goes down this hallway. And we have to keep out of sight of Ms. Penscher so we don't remind her that we're here."

That kept us busy all day. We just stood at the edge of the hallway, and even though a couple of grown-ups saw us, they just complimented us because it was so "cute" that we wanted to watch Election Day. I even ran home and snuck back some lunch so that we wouldn't leave the hallway unguarded.

It was exhausting, and scary, and more than a little boring.

Late in the afternoon, I saw Ms. Penscher notice us as she walked by in the gym. She walked over.

"You kids are still here? Didn't I tell you to leave?"

"No, Ms. Penscher," we said together, like we were singing a song we had practiced. It was true; she had never actually told us to go.

Then she remembered that we had seen Mr. Hartoonian earlier. "You didn't see Mr. Hartoonian again today, did you?"

"No, Ms. Penscher," we said together again.

"Strange," she replied. "He was supposed to be here today, but I never did see him. He opened the building up, and let you in, but after that he was invisible."

"Yes, Ms. Penscher," I sang back to her, but this time Brian and Violet didn't say it with me.

"Well, it's well past time for you kids to be getting home."

"Okay, Ms. Penscher," I said. "Thank you for allowing us to witness the democratic process." I was really laying it on.

She gave me a look like she wasn't sure what I was up to. Which she wasn't.

"Now what?" Violet whispered once Ms. Penscher left us.

"We have to let him out!" Brian said.

"Are you crazy?" I said, way too loudly, causing some of the voting grown-ups to look over in our direction.

"We can't leave him in there!" Brian whispered. "Even if he is a ghost, which I'm starting to think he is not, it's obvious that he doesn't have the power to get out."

"But when we let him out, if he's a ghost he'll haunt us to death! And if he's not a ghost, he'll have the police put us in jail for locking him in a closet all day!"

"We've got to do it," Brian said.

"We've got to do it," Violet agreed.

We went back around the corner. There was no sound. Mr. Hartoonian had either gotten out or given up yelling.

"Okay," I said. "We untie the jump rope, and then run out of here as fast as we can."

"Wait!" Brian said, and he ran off down the hall.

Violet and I looked at each other. In about a minute, Brian came running back.

"I just wanted to wash my hands," he panted. "In case something happens to us and I'm not able to later."

"Okaaay," I said to him.

We put our equipment and backpacks on and quietly began untying the jump rope, and once it was fully untied, WE RAN OUT OF THE HALLWAY AND OUT THROUGH THE GYM AS FAST AS WE COULD.

We ran across the playground and hid behind the jungle gym, which isn't hiding at all because you can see right through it. We watched the door to the school.

Everything looked normal. There was no explosion of angry ghostly howlings. The roof didn't come off the building, with Mr. Hartoonian's spirit leading an army of ghosts to get us. Police cars didn't show up with their sirens blaring.

All we saw was the usual grown-ups walking in and out.

Finally, Mr. Hartoonian came walking slowly out of the building.

PART THIRTEEN

THE PART WHERE WE GET REALLY CONFUSED AND REALIZE THAT WE ABSOLUTELY, TOTALLY, NO-DOUBT-ABOUT-IT DID <u>NOT</u> DEFEAT A GHOST

When Mr. Hartoonian came out of the school, he didn't look like a furious ghost. He looked like a sad man.

We watched him walk past all the grown-ups milling around outside and walk to the bench by the bicycle rack. And then he just sat there.

"Okay," I said. "We did it. And he's not coming after us. Let's get out of here."

"Wait." Brian stared closely at Mr. Hartoonian from behind the jungle gym. "Something's wrong."

"Of course something's wrong . . . for HIM! We stopped him from destroying whatever he wanted to destroy! Mission accomplished. Let's go celebrate."

Brian looked at me. "We've got to go talk to him."

"He's either a ghost or something <u>like</u> a ghost that we locked in a closet for a day! We are not going to walk right up to him!"

"I've got to." Brian walked out from behind the jungle gym and started walking toward him.

"Brian! What are you doing?!" I whisper-shouted at him. Then Violet followed him.

"Oh, of all the spelunking . . ." I said to myself, and I went with them.

We walked right up to Mr. Hartoonian, who looked up at us with a blank expression.

"You're not a ghost," Brian said.

"You are having no idea what you've done," Mr. Hartoonian said quietly. Mr. Hartoonian being quiet and sad was sort of creepier than him being a ghost.

"But . . . you're not a ghost?" Violet asked.

"A ghost?" He looked at us like we were crazy. "You children are having done a terrible thing," Mr. Hartoonian said.

It was hard to stay angry at a guy who was so sad, but I tried to gather up my fury and said, "No, we stopped <u>you</u> from doing a terrible thing! You were going to destroy the school!"

He looked at me with the saddest eyes. I thought he was going to <u>cry</u>! "No, I was just going to use the bat of the baseball to be destroying the fuse box for the school. It would be shutting down the electrical system, there would be no voting on this Election Day at this school, and then I would be <u>leave and go home</u>!"

"Wait, wait," Brian said. Everything was so confusing. "Why would you want to stop the voting?"

Mr. Hartoonian put his face in his hands. This was one sad dude. "I don't know."

Violet spoke up, "What do you mean, <u>you don't know?</u>"

Mr. Hartoonian looked right at Violet. Then he gathered himself up, cleared his throat, and looked at all of us. "All I know is that it was being very important that I stop the voting. The most important thing in the world." Mr. Hartoonian stood up.

This was weird. Okay, he wasn't a ghost, but he wasn't even a bad guy?

Did that mean that <u>we</u> were the bad guys in this story?

OFFICIAL EMU CLUB REPORT
PART FOURTEEN
THE PART WHERE WE FIND OUT THAT <u>WE ARE THE BAD GUYS IN THIS STORY</u>

Mr. Hartoonian said, "You silly children, I am not being a ghost!"

Brian said, "No, you're not. You're a time-traveler."

Had Brian gone bananas? Maybe Mr. Hartoonian wasn't a ghost . . . but a time-traveler??

Mr. Hartoonian looked at Brian. "I might as well tell you. It is not mattering anymore, anyway. Yes, I am being a time-traveler. I'm from your future."

"YOU'RE A TIME-TRAVELER??" I yelled.

"Shhh!" Mr. Hartoonian urged me, looking back at the grown-ups at the school, who totally didn't hear me.

"You're not a ghost who is haunting the school?" Violet asked.

"There is being no such thing as ghosts," Mr. Hartoonian said.

"He's a time-traveler," Brian said. "That's why he can appear out of thin air. And it must have something to do with time going really slowly near the maintenance closet."

Mr. Hartoonian said sort of impatiently, "Yes, yes. That closet is a natural time portal. It's a place where time-travelers can travel to and from, and it is causes pulsating time disruptions."

Brian said, "So the closet creates time disturbances that slow down time at certain times of the day?"

"Yes," Mr. Hartoonian said, sadly. "We time-travelers use these portals to travel between time periods."

This didn't seem likely to me. "You're a janitor!" I said.

"I am being full of surprises." Mr. Hartoonian managed a small smile. "To being specific, I am a

Time Event Manipulator. See, what happens is, scientists in the future figure out what things in the past caused bad things to happen. I go back in time, and I will do what they've told me. The things they are telling me to do in the past will be causing <u>good</u> things to happen in the future."

"So you fix and clean things up in the past so everything will be good in the future," I said.

"That is being right."

"So, you're a Time Janitor!" I said.

"I am being a Time Event Manipulator!"

"Did you once go back to the time when President Franklin Roosevelt was a young man?" Brian asked.

"Why, yes, I did," Mr. Hartoonian said, surprised. "My mission was being to hand him a chocolate bar. That was a favorite mission of mine. It is being kind of a hobby of mine to meet future world leaders."

Then Mr. Hartoonian frowned. "How did you know I met him?" he asked Brian.

"There was a picture of you with him in Stuart's social studies book," Brian said.

"Oh." Mr. Hartoonian looked concerned. "That is not supposed to happen."

"You're not very good at your job, are you?" I said.

Mr. Hartoonian shot me a look. Then he sighed. "Well, I failed in this mission. I was being sent to this time to make sure voting didn't happen at this school on this day. And it did."

Brian asked, "And what bad thing in the future were you trying to avoid?"

Mr. Hartoonian looked away. "A war. A really big war. A world war."

Violet asked, "How can voting here cause a really big war?"

Mr. Hartoonian sat down again. "Well, like I said, I am not knowing how. Scientists figure out the mission and I am just doing it. Probably someone is getting elected and that causes something, which causes something else, which causes something else. Little things, even little _good_ things, can be leading to big things, sometimes big, <u>bad</u> things."

"Wow," Brian said. "So . . ." He didn't finish.

"Yes," Mr. Hartoonian said. "I failed, so there will be a terrible war."

Gulp. We thought Mr. Hartoonian was a ghost. And because we were wrong, there's going to be a huge WAR?

Brian said, "Why can't the future scientists just send someone else back. Like, to yesterday, and try again?"

An angry look shot across Mr. Hartoonian's face. "You think maybe time-traveling across decades and the centuries is like getting in your car and going to the store to get some milk?! We get one chance. One!"

"Can't you do <u>something</u>?" I asked.

"I can't do anything. I can't stop the war. I can't even be getting home to the future."

"Why not?" Brian asked.

Mr. Hartoonian took a small metal thing from his coat pocket. It was the metal toy we broke when we trapped Mr. Hartoonian in the closet.

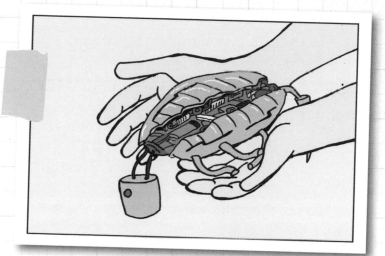

"<u>This</u> is being my time machine. It is attaching to my arm, and I am using it in the time portal. But this isn't taking me anywhere. Ever. I am being stuck in this time, and I can't stop the war."

He tossed his broken time machine down onto the ground.

Oh, boy. We had really done it. We thought our really cool club was going to save the school.

Instead, our horrible club DOOMED THE EARTH.

OFFICIAL EMU CLUB REPORT

PART FIFTEEN
THE PART WHERE WE JUST MIGHT TOTALLY SAVE THE DAY—AND PROBABLY SEVERAL CENTURIES

I picked up the little time machine. "You don't know how to fix this?"

"I don't think it can be fixed even if I were being home in the future. But if it can be fixed, I'm not someone who can do it. I'm a Time Event Manipulator, not a mechanic."

I said, "Well, I know someone who is better than a mechanic."

"Is that being right? Who?" Mr. Hartoonian said, without looking up, not at all believing me.

"My dog."

Brian smiled. "That's right!"

Mr. Hartoonian looked at me, with his head tilted down, like he was talking to a baby. "Look, you crazy, ridiculous boy. I am being from the future, so I would know: There is being no such thing as ghosts, and there is being no such thing as genius mechanic dogs."

"There is!" Brian said.

I asked Mr. Hartoonian, "Can I take this? We'll be right back."

"It is garbage now. I have failed, and I am being lost forever in this time. Go ahead."

"Come on!" I said to Brian and Violet, and we started jogging toward my house.

As we jogged, I said to Brian, "It's a good thing I got us to go talk to Mr. Hartoonian and find out what's going on, instead of just running away."

Brian snorted. "What? You're the one who wanted to run away. It was _my_ idea to talk to him."

"Come on, Brian," I said. "A good leader always makes it _seem_ like his followers come up with the plans _he_ wants to do."

"You're not the leader of the EMU Club!" Brian said. He's so naïve. "And anyway," he continued, "by telling me that, you're <u>not</u> making it seem like it was my idea."

Suddenly I realized we really had to hurry. "Come on, you two!" I barked. "We've got to move it!"

When we got home, my parents were in the kitchen making dinner. "Did you have fun watching the voting?" my dad called out as we walked in the front door.

"Yeah, Dad," I called back, out of breath, and we ran through to the backyard to find Ferdinand.

"Ferdinand! Come here, boy!" Ferdinand came running out of his doghouse like any normal dog and jumped on me and Violet.

I took the broken time machine out of my pocket. "Look, Ferdinand. Can you fix this?"

Ferdinand stopped his slobbering, stood up on two legs (yes, he can stand on two legs), and looked carefully at the time machine.

He took it from me and examined its exposed insides, cocking his head this way and that. This thing definitely interested him.

As I said earlier in this report, Ferdinand is a robot who was put on Earth by evil aliens thousands of years ago (see: First Official Report of the EMU Club). But he's a good dog.

Ferdinand put the time machine in his mouth and ran on all fours into the house. We quietly followed him into the den, where we found him sitting in the chair at my dad's desk, his paw on the laptop computer, whining.

Oh, boy. I knew exactly what he was saying. He was going to need parts from the laptop in order to fix the time machine.

I looked at Violet. "Dad's going to be so disappointed when he finds out his new laptop doesn't work," I whispered.

Violet nodded sadly. "It's for a good cause."

I whispered, "The best cause. We're trying to save millions, maybe <u>billions</u> of future lives!"

I gave Ferdinand the go-ahead. He ran to bring tools from the garage and then he started taking the laptop apart.

It was amazing to watch him work. He knew exactly what to do (or it seemed that way), and he worked super fast.

After a few minutes, Ferdinand closed up the laptop so that it <u>looked</u> like it did before (there was no way the laptop was going to <u>work</u> like it did before, though), and he sort of whined as he pushed the time machine over to me.

"Did you fix the time machine, Ferdinand?" I asked him.

He gave a noncommittal bark. I decided to give him the benefit of the doubt. "Good boy!" I rubbed his head.

We ran into the kitchen. Mom was stirring something on the stove, and Dad was setting the table. "I forgot my book at school. I have to run back and get it."

Mom said, "Oh, Stuart. Dinner's in about ten minutes."

"That's plenty of time," I said, smiling at Brian. If this thing worked, time would be on our side.

"Be careful," she called as we all ran out the backdoor, including Ferdinand.

PART SIXTEEN

THE PART WHERE WE ACTUALLY, REALLY, HONESTLY DO TRAVEL THROUGH TIME!!! AND WE FIND OUT WHAT A BATTLE DRONE IS (AND IT'S NOT GOOD)!

As we got to school, it was just starting to get dark. We ran down the driveway, and then I saw them.

Bradley Ketchum with Arthur Barnes and Ricky Buscema, on their bikes, cruising up and down the driveway.

I barely looked at them.

But that didn't stop Bradley from passing a comment. "Hey, look who's running to school," he said to Arthur and Ricky, but really to me. "I didn't know baloney was <u>fast food</u>."

What a lame joke. But Arthur and Ricky laughed.

I'm on a desperate mission to save the future of our planet, and I have to put up with <u>that</u>. We kept running toward the side of the school by the playground, where we had left Mr. Hartoonian.

We found him still slumped on the same bench where we had left him.

"What is it being <u>now</u>?" he asked when we approached him. He was not happy to see us.

I held out the time machine and pointed to Ferdinand. "He fixed it."

Mr. Hartoonian took the time machine and looked mildly surprised. He rolled up his sleeve and placed the machine on his forearm. It's six dangling legs suddenly sprung to life and wrapped themselves around his arm. The body lit up.

"Wha . . . ? How did you be doing this?" he sputtered. He was shocked. "What kind of dog is this?"

Brian said, "An alien robot dog."

I said, "I am being full of surprises."

Mr. Hartoonian looked at the time machine carefully, pressing various buttons. "Astounding! The V-ChronoStabilizer is shot and the Micro Particle Collider will be totally unstable, but it might be doing <u>something</u> useful."

"I told you. My dog is a spelunking genius," I said proudly to Mr. Hartoonian. I dropped in the "spelunking" to see if I could get a clue from Mr. Hartoonian that my word will be really popular in the future.

"What is this 'spelunking' you say? Isn't that cave exploring?" Mr. Hartoonian asked, still examining the machine.

"Never mind." I frowned. Apparently, I've still got my work cut out for me.

Violet asked, "Mr. Hartoonian, will it work?"

"We'll have to go to the portal to see,"
Mr. Hartoonian said, still marveling at the repaired
time machine.

"The maintenance closet," Brian said.

Mr. Hartoonian had all the school keys, so it
was easy to go into the school by a side entrance
where we wouldn't be noticed by the grown-ups,
who were still voting. He couldn't take his eyes off
the time machine. "This will be very unpredictable.
I'll be having very little control over what it does.
But it's a chance we've got to be taking."

As we ran upstairs, I asked Mr. Hartoonian,
"What kind of accent do you have? You say your
sentences weird."

"It is being a thing from the future. Even
English-speakers from your past would be
saying you talk 'weird.'"

Wow, he didn't have a foreign accent. He had a
<u>future</u> accent.

We ran up to the maintenance closet. We all
squeezed in, and Mr. Hartoonian started furiously
working the controls on the time machine on
his forearm.

"I may be needing you to come with me. I have no idea how this is going to be working," Mr. Hartoonian said. "It may be dangerous."

"What do we do?" asked Brian. We knew we had to help.

"Stay close to me. A Wormhole Sphere is going to form around us." The closet could barely fit us all. Staying close to him was not a problem.

And just as he said it, suddenly we were all standing inside a large glowing ball that we could see through. It was like we were hamsters in one of those plastic balls they run around in. But this ball looked like it was made out of glowing water or something.

Ferdinand barked.

And there was a loud buzzing sound.

We couldn't get a picture of the bubble because we were inside it, so I drew this picture of what it must have looked like from the outside.

Mr. Hartoonian started working his controls.

"Be hanging on. I'm not sure what's going to happen," he said.

Suddenly we weren't in the maintenance closet anymore. We were still in the sphere, but it was in a field, with some trees in the distance, and the sun was setting.

Violet was taking pictures.

"Be hanging on, and stay together," Mr. Hartoonian warned us.

Then suddenly our bubble was in a city, with people walking past us. But they were wearing weird clothes and the buildings looked strange. The people were ignoring us and walking right through the bubble and us, like we didn't really exist. And they couldn't even hear the crazy-loud buzzing. It was like we could see them, but they couldn't see or feel us at all.

"This is being crazy," Mr. Hartoonian yelled above the buzzing. "I can't be controlling where we go, and we aren't fully forming. It's like . . ."

"It's like we're ghosts!" I finished for him.

Then suddenly our bubble was in some kind of swamp.

Then we were in a horrible place. Everything was black and smoky, and there were explosions you could see off on the horizon.

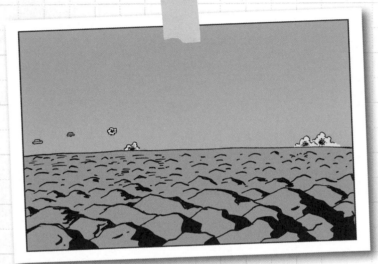

A terrible thought crossed my mind. Could we be looking at the future war we were trying to stop from happening?

"Oh, no!"

Of all the sentences you could hear a Time Janitor say when you're inside a bubble that is currently at the most horrible war in the history of the future, "Oh, no!" is one of the very worst.

"What's wrong, Mr. Hartoonian?" Brian asked.

Before Mr. Hartoonian could answer, the bubble was suddenly GONE!

"Let's get out of here!" I yelled to Mr. Hartoonian.

"I am being to trying!!!" he yelled back. This place was in the future for him, too, and I think it was freaking him out.

Mr. Hartoonian was frantically fiddling with the controls of the device on his forearm.

He said, "The Wormhole Sphere that transports us needs just the right atmospheric density, and it is being hard to change the settings on this time machine which you have been hitting with a baseball bat!"

"Great," I thought, "so now he got us stuck in a war zone, and he's blaming me."

Brian said, through his coughs, "Look!"

He pointed way off in the distance, where some kind of flying thing was coming toward us.

Mr. Hartoonian said, "A Battle Drone! Its sensors must have being picking up our presence! We've got to be getting out of here, being fast!" His weird way of talking, with all those extra words, sure wasn't speeding things up.

The Battle Drone, whatever that was, was getting closer. I could see that it was sort of like a windowless flying car, but it didn't look friendly.

It was getting hard to breathe. Violet coughed. Brian was coughing so hard, he stumbled forward.

"THERE!" Mr. Hartoonian said.

The bubble appeared around us again, and the buzzing sound started again. We were all safe. Except . . .

"BRIAN!" shouted Violet.

He wasn't in the bubble; we could see him just outside it.

We were all just standing on the black, rocky ground, and the air was hard to breathe. The buzzing sound of the bubble was gone, and it was quiet, except for the explosions we could see and hear in the distance.

Then Brian started coughing.

I picked up Ferdinand, who was having trouble standing on the rocks . . .

OFFICIAL EMU CLUB REPORT

PART SEVENTEEN
THE PART WHERE WE TOTALLY ESCAPE THE WAR AND THEN I WRITE A NOTE TO MYSELF

"TURN OFF THE SPHERE! WE'VE GOT TO GET BRIAN," I yelled.

"I CAN'T," Mr. Hartoonian yelled back over the buzzing. "I WON'T BE ABLE TO GET IT BACK UP AGAIN."

The Battle Drone was getting close.

Brian looked around in a panic. He couldn't even see us, even though we were right next to him.

Ferdinand started barking like crazy.

Violet dropped the camera, and it took this picture.

Now, when I do something brilliant, I'll say so. Not because I like to brag; I don't. Just because I'm honest. But here, I can't even say that what I did was brilliant, because I didn't even think of it. <u>I just did it</u>.

I reached into Violet's backpack and got out the Dustbuster, the little vacuum cleaner she was going to use to trap a ghost.

I put it up to a spot on the wall of the bubble closest to Brian and turned it on.

The spot on the bubble shimmered and shook, and I could tell the wall had become very thin.

The Battle Drone was almost at Brian.

I reached through the wall, outside the bubble, grabbed Brian's arm, and pulled with all my strength.

He shot into the bubble, and suddenly we were gone from that horrible place. All of us!

"YOU ARE DID IT!!" Mr. Hartoonian cheered.

"Brian, are you okay??" Violet asked.

"Yes," he coughed.

Our bubble was now in a town, and the people were dressed like in an old movie. It looked like my town, but all the stores were different, and everyone looked old-fashioned.

Best of all, it was peaceful.

Mr. Hartoonian said to me, "Amazing! Your vacuum device was disrupting the atmospheric pressure just enough to be creating a permeable area—"

"WE'VE GOT TO GET HOME," I interrupted, shouting at him. I'd had enough of this time bouncing. And the horrible air that had gotten into the bubble at the war zone was making my eyes tear up.

"I'm trying to ... If I can just get us to a few days before ..." Mr. Hartoonian was sweating as he worked the controls on the time machine.

Then we were in MY BACKYARD!

BEHIND MY TREE!

AND THERE, SITTING ON THE SWINGS, WERE ME AND BRIAN!!

"Hold it!" I yelled to Mr. Hartoonian. "You did it! It's just a few months ago! We can do something to help here!"

"I can't keep us here for long," he said through gritted teeth, as he worked a joystick thingy. "It's very difficult to stabilize . . ."

Brian, still coughing, managed to say, "This is us, during the summer, before school started, when we were trying to think of a mystery!"

Violet shouted, "You've got to tell yourselves not to interfere with Mr. Hartoonian! To leave him alone and let him do his mission!"

"I've got an idea!" I yelled, and I took off my backpack and took out a piece of paper.

I kneeled down and began writing.

"That may work!" Mr. Hartoonian yelled over the buzzing. "If you use your air disruptor, we might be able to be getting a piece of paper out of the Wormhole Sphere."

I finished the note.

"HURRY! I CAN'T HOLD US HERE MUCH LONGER! THE WORMHOLE SPHERE MAY DISSOLVE AGAIN!" Mr. Hartoonian shouted. Now he was on his knees from the effort.

"TRY TO SLIDE THE PAPER THROUGH THE WORMHOLE SPHERE."

I held the Dustbuster up to the bubble wall, and Brian put the paper next to it.

"Wait!" I said. "I have to write a P.S.!"

"A P.S.?!!" Brian yelled. "Are you nuts?"

I grabbed the paper back and dropped back to my knees to add something to the note.

"Okay! Let's do it," I yelled. The buzzing was getting louder and louder.

"DO IT!!" yelled Mr. Hartoonian.

I turned on the Dustbuster, and Brian and Violet tried to slide the note through. It was working. We were slowly sliding it out of the bubble.

As we did it, I looked out of the bubble and saw Ferdinand running across the yard toward us. Yet there he was right next to us in the bubble. Did Past–Ferdinand somehow see us?

The Ferdinand next to me in the bubble barked.

The Ferdinand running across the yard barked.

"That dog can be seeing in four dimensions!" Mr. Hartoonian said. Whatever that means.

The Ferdinand in the yard took a running leap at the bubble, like he wanted to jump into my arms.

I kept pushing the paper out. "NO, FERDINAND!"

Then, ZAP!

We were out of my yard and back in the maintenance closet.

The bubble was still around us, but the buzzing wasn't as loud. I was holding the last part of the paper that didn't make it through. I looked at the torn scrap, and was relieved to see that it was just a corner, and that everything I had written had gotten out. I put the scrap in my pocket.

Mr. Hartoonian said, "I've got only a few seconds. You can be getting out here more easily because we're at a portal. I think I can make it home to my future."

I said, "Good-bye, Mr. Hartoonian! I'm really sorry we stopped your mission and may have caused a world war."

Brian said, "Bye! Soon you'll know if we were successful . . . You'll either go home to a war that's starting, or to peace."

The buzzing was getting louder. "Hurry!" he shouted, and we went up to the edge of the sphere.

The buzzing was getting very loud as I turned on the Dustbuster and held it up to the bubble's wall again. Brian picked up Ferdinand and was able to push his way out.

Violet said, "Bye, Mr. Hartoonian."

The buzzing was super loud, but Mr. Hartoonian looked right into Violet's eyes, and I thought I heard him say, "Good-bye, Violet. It was an honor to have met you." I have no idea what that was supposed to mean.

She pushed through the bubble, then I did . . .

And then POP.

Brian, Violet, Ferdinand, and I were sitting in an ordinary maintenance closet. No bubble. No buzzing. No Mr. Hartoonian.

You would expect a maintenance closet in a school at the end of a day to be very quiet, but after everything that had just happened, it was strange for the four of us to just be sitting there in silence.

I said, "That was un-spelunking-believable."

Brian went into the boys' room to wash his hands, and this time I went, too.

We walked out of the maintenance closet and down toward the gym.

There was no one in the gym, and it was dark. The sun outside was still setting, as if no time had passed.

As we left the gym out to the school driveway, we saw a fire engine and two police cars parked.

There was a big handwritten sign on the door to the school. "Voting cancelled at this location due to power outage."

Grown-ups were talking at the door, and some were angry, because they were being turned away and would have to vote somewhere else, or maybe they wouldn't vote at all.

We had done it! Mr. Hartoonian was able to stop the voting here, and somehow, in some crazy way, that stopped a world war from happening far in the future.

We were standing on the sidewalk, staring at the school, when I saw Bradley Ketchum and Arthur and Ricky riding their bikes toward us.

I didn't even care what Bradley Ketchum said to me, I was so happy and relieved.

But he didn't say anything. Arthur and Ricky said, "Hi, Stuart."

"Um . . . Hi, guys."

After they passed, Brian said, "I thought everyone was calling you Baloney this year."

I smiled.

PART EIGHTEEN
THE PART WHERE EVERYTHING IS STRANGELY NORMAL

We got home, and Mom said, "Hi, kids. Get washed up for dinner." Like everything was totally normal, and we didn't just cause and then prevent a world war.

My dad said, "Brian, do you want to stay for dinner? I could call your mom."

Brian said, "No, thanks, Mr. Tennemeier. I'd better be getting home. I've had an extra-long day. But before I go, can I just . . ."

"Sure," my dad said. "You can wash your hands."

The three of us walked upstairs. We were still so shocked, we didn't feel like talking. We went into my room. I wanted to get to dinner (now I was starving), but I had to do something first.

I looked on my desk. It looked the same . . . except I looked closely, and there was a piece of paper sticking out from under my social studies book. I pulled it out. Then I took the scrap of paper in my pocket and put it next to it. Violet took a picture.

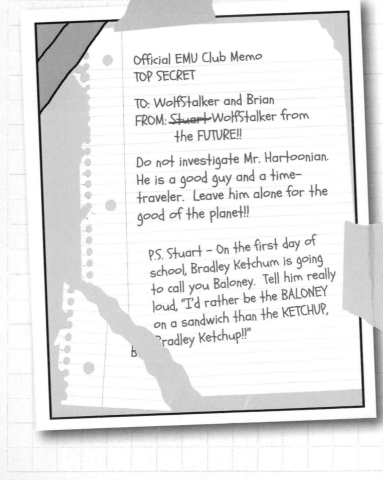

Official EMU Club Memo
TOP SECRET

TO: WolfStalker and Brian
FROM: ~~Stuart~~ WolfStalker from
      the FUTURE!!

Do not investigate Mr. Hartoonian. He is a good guy and a time-traveler. Leave him alone for the good of the planet!!

P.S. Stuart - On the first day of school, Bradley Ketchum is going to call you Baloney. Tell him really loud, "I'd rather be the BALONEY on a sandwich than the KETCHUP, Bradley Ketchup!!"

I wish I could have been there on the first day of school when I shot Bradley Ketchum that comeback, so that I could hear everyone laugh.

Actually, I guess I was.

Anyway, after a quick, funny comeback like that, there was no way the Baloney nickname was going to stick to me.

"Wow," Brian said.

I smiled at him.

"I'm going to go wash my hands now."

"Sure."

He walked to my bathroom, then turned around to face me.

He said, "Hey, WolfStalker."

"Yeah?"

"Thanks for saving me."

I gave him a salute.

OFFICIAL EMU CLUB REPORT
PART NINETEEN
THE LAST PART

So it turns out we didn't have an adventure after all. Here's the way it all went now: We were on the swings, trying to think of a mystery. We found a mysterious message from Future Me. And so we <u>didn't</u> investigate Mr. Hartoonian, and we <u>didn't</u> stop him from preventing a world war.

Except the members of the EMU Club remember it slightly differently.

The way the EMU Club remembers it is that we wanted to find out why time went so slowly in my classroom at the end of the day. And we discovered that the reason is that there was a time-traveler from the future whose mission was to save the future Earth.

It's all very confusing.

For example, does this conclude my Official Report on our second mystery?

Or was there <u>no mystery at all</u>?

SCIENCE FACTS ABOUT EMUS

BY STUART TENNEMEIER, President, EMU Club

The emu is the official mascot of the <u>E</u>xploration <u>M</u>ystery <u>U</u>nbelievable Club, for obvious reasons.

But did you know there are lots of fun science facts about emus?

There are.

In fact, there are more fun science facts about emus than any other animal!

Emus can run up to 100 miles per hour.

ZOOM

131

Fierce fighters, emus have been known to
protect elephants from poachers.

Many consider the emu to be the smartest of
all animals. One emu was taught a vocabulary of
1,000 words in sign language, using its beak.

← "Sphere"

The rarest kind of emu is the tigmu, which is a combination of a tiger and an emu.

Native Australians worship emus as gods. It is illegal in Australia to make fun of emus.

Emus are descended from Tyrannosaurus Rex. "Emu" is actually a caveman word, meaning "King of All Dinosaurs."

Stuart-

None of this is true. You made it all up.

- Brian

TIME JANITOR

WHAT DOES A TIME JANITOR DO?

Brian and I don't really understand this (although Brian says he does!). But basically, we think Time Janitors go back in time to "clean up" certain things that happen that cause bad things to happen in the future.

How can that work? See, little things can cause really, really big things. Brian told me about a famous example of a butterfly in a jungle.

Let's say there's this one tiny butterfly in the jungle and he decides to flap his wings once. That may seem like no big deal.

But it might cause just a LITTLE BIT more wind going in a certain direction, which could cause a cloud to move a little bit more quickly, which could cause it to join with other rain clouds, which could cause a storm moving over the ocean, which could be the reason you got a Snow Day off from school!

And on that Snow Day you might build a snow fort, and then fall down into the fort and get snow down your pants, which causes you to catch a cold, and so you stay home sick the next day and miss the day the parts are given out for the school play.

So it's all that stupid butterfly's fault that you're playing a tree in "The Sound of Music."

If I could go back in time and stop that butterfly from flapping its wings, maybe I could be an actual human person in the play, and I wouldn't have to spend a half-hour on stage in a smelly cardboard tube listening to Angela Montgomery sing "Sixteen Going on Seventeen."

And if I could, I would.

THE ADVENTURES CONTINUE!

Coming soon!
The next EMU
Club ~~mystery!~~
exploration!

ABOUT THE AUTHOR

Ruben Bolling is the author of the award-winning weekly comic strip *Tom the Dancing Bug,* **which features characters like a pre-historic ape-man, an idiot time-traveler, and a talking duck. And sometimes weird characters, like politicians.**

He is the president of the Mystery Club, which was founded when he was eight years old with his friend, Mike. The Club's first mystery is still an open case.

ACKNOWLEDGMENTS

I'd like to thank Andrea Colvin, Shelly Barkes, Jean Lucas, and the whole spelunking gang at Andrews McMeel. I want to thank Jason Yarn, and of course I thank Adam Rex for making the cover of this book a second masterpiece.

I thank my great friends and my family: my parents, my brothers, and sisters-in-law and their families; and my kids Katie, Jake, and Zoe who made me tell them countless Monopoly Jr. stories. And I thank my wife, Andrea, always.

I dedicate this book to everyone who read and loved *Alien Invasion in My Backyard*. All the teachers, librarians, booksellers, grownups, and (especially) kids who took Stuart, Brian, Violet, and Ferdinand into their hearts are the real heroes of the proud and mighty EMU Club!

Andrews McMeel Publishing, LLC
an Andrews McMeel Universal company
1130 Walnut Street, Kansas City, Missouri 64106

www.andrewsmcmeel.com

15 16 17 18 19 SDB 10 9 8 7 6 5 4 3 2 1

ISBN: 978-1-4494-5710-5

Library of Congress Control Number: 2015938220

Made by:
Shenzhen Donnelley Printing Company Ltd.
Address and location of manufacturer:
No. 47, Wuhe Nan Road, Bantian Ind. Zone,
Shenzhen China, 518129
1st Printing—8/3/15

ATTENTION: SCHOOLS AND BUSINESSES

Andrews McMeel books are available at quantity discounts with bulk purchase for educational, business, or sales promotional use. For information, please e-mail the Andrews McMeel Publishing Special Sales Department: specialsales@amuniversal.com.

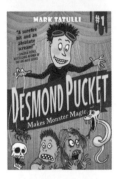

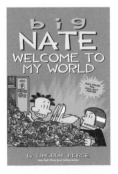